Salty Splashes

C O L L E C T I O N™

Salty Splashes

COLLECTION™

Salty Splashes
COLLECTION™

Isle of Mystery
EYES OF THE KING

JZ Bingham

Illustrations by Curt Walstead

Balcony 7 Media and Publishing

SANTA BARBARA, CALIFORNIA

Printed in the United States of America

ISBN: 978-1-939454-12-6
Library of Congress Control Number: 2012955082

Additional copies of this book, including bulk orders, are
available at www.balcony7.com

Published by Balcony 7 Media and Publishing LLC
133 East De La Guerra St., #177
Santa Barbara, CA 93101
(805) 679-1821
info@balcony7.com
www.balcony7.com

Printed by Lehigh Phoenix

Book Design and Production by DesignForBooks.com
Art Direction, Character and Storyboard Development: Balcony 7 Studios
Cover Art and Interior Illustrations: Curt Walstead

To the simple joy of innocence . . .

May it never end . . .

Salty Splashes
COLLECTION™

www.saltysplashes.com

Follow, Share, Visit And Connect With Us
Learn About The Excitement

Also by J.Z. Bingham

Dreamy Drums, Trouble in Paradise

Gansevort, The King and His Court

A Salty Splashes Collection™

Introduction

Welcome to the *Salty Splashes Collection*™, a world of illustrated fiction for children. *Salty Splashes* tales are told in playful rhymes which are lots of fun to read by kids, as well as adults. Meet our lovable cartoon cast: a precocious bunch who seem to find trouble wherever they go; but they always stick together and learn important lessons along the way. You can meet new characters in every story and join in their antics and adventure. *Salty Splashes* books are in a numbered series but can be enjoyed in any order.

Children of all ages will love these stories because the colorful, detailed illustrations describe every scene and make learning words easier and more exciting.

A balance of easy and more difficult words will help kids expand their vocabulary. Story time is more fun with our mix of narrative and character dialogue because kids can engage in role play, all in rhyme.

Isle of Mystery is the second book in the *Salty Splashes Collection*™. Our cartoon characters find themselves exploring a mysterious island. The storyboard designs of Balcony 7 Studios, combined with the hand-drawn illustrations of Curt Walstead, help bring the characters and their cartoon world to life. With every turn of the page, and with every twist in the story, you will almost hear their voices come to life as well. Stay tuned . . . Soon, you actually will . . .

〜 J.Z. Bingham

It was a wicked storm that brought them to this patch of sand.
They felt like brave explorers in a far away land.
As they looked around this empty isle of mystery,
They came upon a sign that seemed real old and eerie.

"What do you think it says?" Melrose asked with a frown.
"It says whoever lives here doesn't want us around!"
Kat looked up the beach and saw a scary crab.
Then a snake emerged; his tongue gave the air a jab.

"Yikes!" Sammy cried, "What's with these gnarly trees?"
"They're so weird!" Kat agreed, "They're giving me the willies!"

Just then the wind picked up; the trees began to shake.
The branches leaned as if their trunks had come awake.
They decided they should run from these clutches of bark,
To try and find some shelter; it was quickly
    getting dark.

"Hey, check this out! Looks like a path someone made."
They followed Sammy's lead toward a canopy of shade.
"It's getting kind of chilly," Kat replied with a frown.
"We should find a place to camp." She started looking around.

"That's a fine idea!" Wiggleworm agreed.
He started inching toward a log, "I think I found what I need!"
Kat rolled her eyes, "That's not exactly what I meant!
Explorers like us need a nice cozy tent!"

"A tent! That's it!" Sammy cried excitedly.
"Like with leaves and wooden stakes! A toasty fire maybe?"

"A fire would be grand," Wiggleworm declared.
"And what would you suggest we light it with?" Kat stared.

"That's a good point," Melrose said with a frown.
"I guess we could just pile a bunch of leaves on the ground . . ."

"Well, we have no choice. Let's get to work," she said.
"Let's split up and gather just enough to make a bed."

Sammy made his way along a path toward some shrubs.
As he lifted dead leaves, he uncovered slimy grubs!
"Cool!" he stared in awe, and they stared right back.
But he quickly jumped aside as they stood up to attack!
Sammy dropped the leaves to make a quick escape,
When he spotted Wiggleworm with his mouth agape.

"Hey, watcha' got there?" Sammy asked quietly.
"I believe I found a member of my lost family!"
Sammy followed his eyes, and to his great surprise,
He found himself staring at a worm with yellow eyes.

"Whoa! He looks like YOU, only more scary and BLUE!
Can he talk? Did you ask if he's related to you?"
"No, he won't talk; he just keeps STARING at me . . ."

Just then the worm stood up and yelled, "JUST LET ME BE!
I was minding MY OWN BUSINESS. Then you BARGED RIGHT IN!
Go somewhere ELSE, I say! This here log is TAKEN!"

"Well, EXCUSE ME!" Wiggleworm shouted back.
"You can HAVE your silly log! You GROUCHY old HACK!"

Not too far away, Kat ripped some bark off a tree.
It would make a perfect bed, she thought, real warm and comfy.
As she ripped another sheet, a branch began to shake.
She looked up just in time to meet the eyes of a snake!

She jumped back; she was startled by its spooky stare.
He hissed at her, "Listen here! You're disturbing my lair!"
She didn't know what to say; she backed away with care.
She gathered up her bark to run away from there!

But Melrose caught her eye; he was staring at the sky.
"Kat! You'll never guess what I just saw fly by!"

"I hope it wasn't a snake, 'cause that's what I just saw!"

"No! A FLYING SQUIRREL!" He pointed up with his paw.

"WHAT? That's so WEIRD! What a SPOOKY place!
Let's try to find the others . . ." Fear was showing on her face.

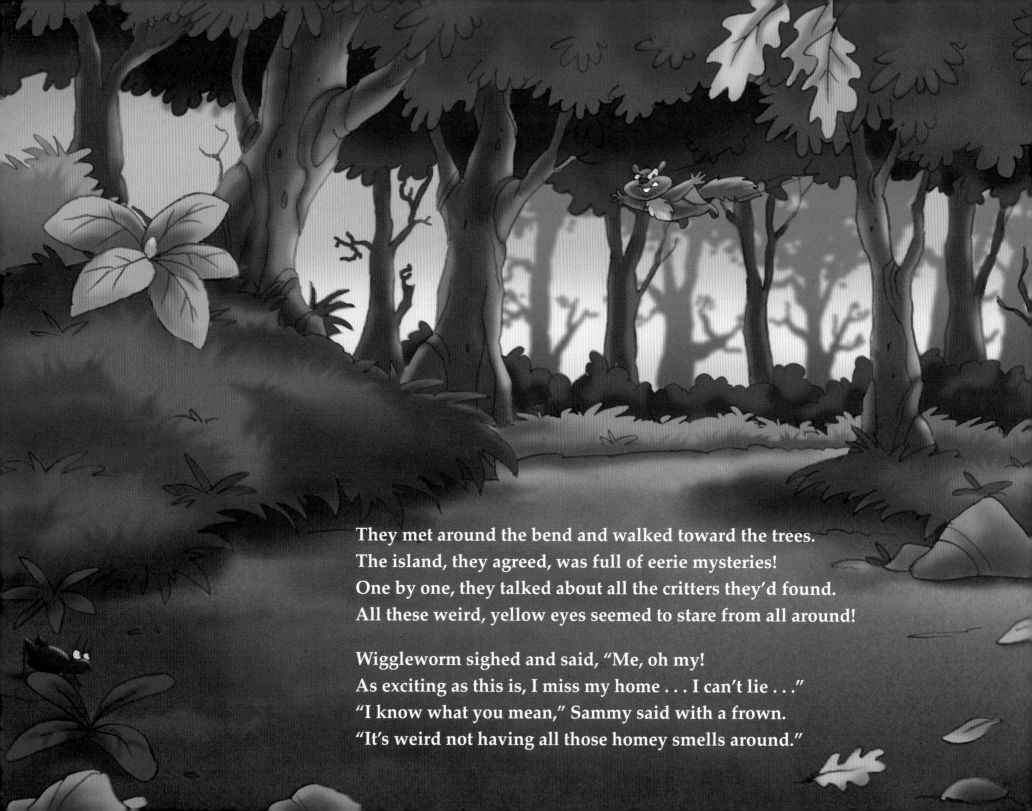

They met around the bend and walked toward the trees.
The island, they agreed, was full of eerie mysteries!
One by one, they talked about all the critters they'd found.
All these weird, yellow eyes seemed to stare from all around!

Wiggleworm sighed and said, "Me, oh my!
As exciting as this is, I miss my home . . . I can't lie . . ."
"I know what you mean," Sammy said with a frown.
"It's weird not having all those homey smells around."

Kat stopped in her tracks, "Mom and Dad!" she cried.
"They must be worried sick 'cause we're still outside!"
Their excitement quickly died, as they sat there side by side.
Back at home, they might be searching for them, far and wide!

Kat was right: Back at home, it became very clear,
That something wasn't right when they didn't appear.
The storm was swift and strong; waves were crashing on the beach.
A group of searchers combed through every dune within reach.

Mom stayed at home, just in case they returned.
The other neighbor Moms came as soon as they learned.
Dad returned with some news, "There's no sign of the four . . .
But a surfer saw them get into a boat on the shore!"

His eyes were bright with hope, "The boat is no longer there!
So Dutch and the storks started to search by air!"
Mom seemed relieved to hear this bit of news.
"We'll find them," Dad declared, "We have no time to lose!"

Meanwhile, on the island, there was more to see.
Our explorers were at work, making progress quietly.
They heard a waterfall and made their way
toward the sound,
Of a crystal clear stream, flowing
strongly toward the ground.

Sammy jumped ahead to take a well-earned drink.
He lapped at falling drops; the splashes made him blink.
The others stared and laughed. Melrose soon joined in.
"Just don't drink the weird fish!" He yelled out with a grin.

Kat and Wiggleworm took a rest on a log.
"At least now we have fresh water, and a real
    happy dog!"
Before she spoke her last word, the worm gasped,
    "What's that?"
She looked over, dropped her jaw and yelled,
    "Yuck! It's a rat!"

Something else caught Sammy's eye, "Hey, who wants to be brave?"
He blinked to be sure, "I think I spotted a cave!"
They approached it carefully, huddled close
and peered inside.
The worm said, "I'll go . . . if Sammy gives me a ride . . ."

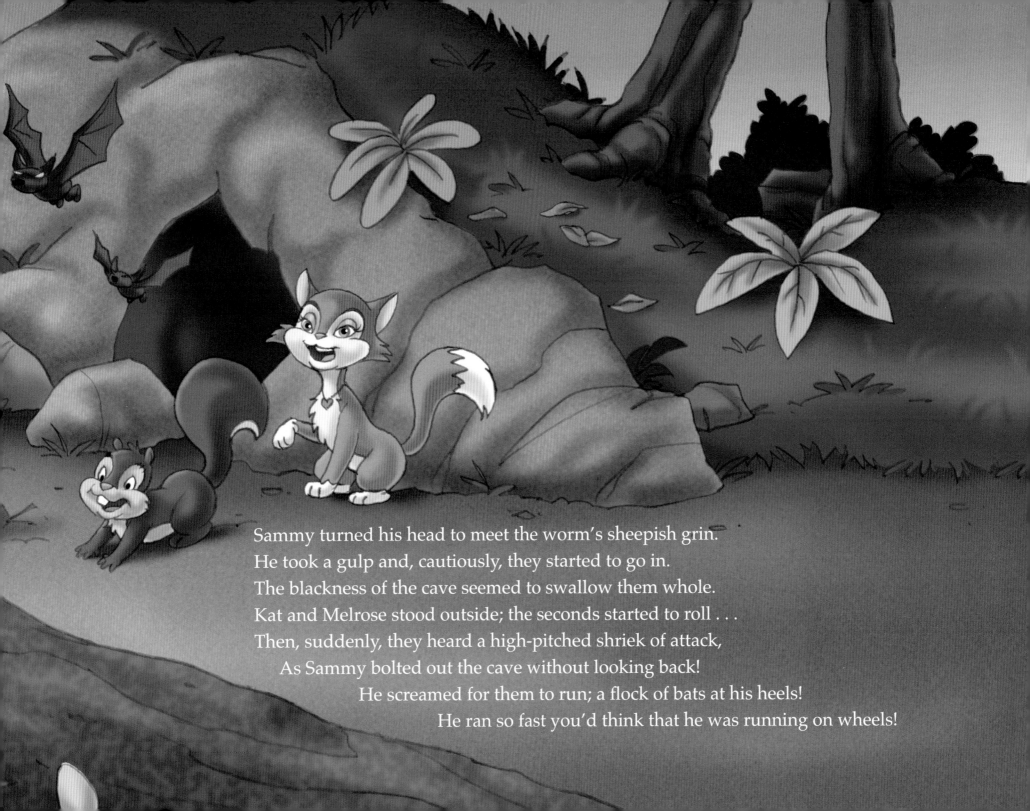

Sammy turned his head to meet the worm's sheepish grin.
He took a gulp and, cautiously, they started to go in.
The blackness of the cave seemed to swallow them whole.
Kat and Melrose stood outside; the seconds started to roll . . .
Then, suddenly, they heard a high-pitched shriek of attack,
As Sammy bolted out the cave without looking back!
He screamed for them to run; a flock of bats at his heels!
He ran so fast you'd think that he was running on wheels!

They ran until they reached a clearing in the trees.
Panting hard, they stopped to feel the cool ocean breeze.
It started first with Kat: a chuckle turned into a laugh.
One by one, they all joined in; their sides were splitting in half!

They caught their breath, and Sammy said, "Okay, here's the plan:
Melrose, you're the scout! Be as quiet as you can!
Take a quick look around, then tell us what you see."

"I don't know . . ." Melrose said, "Why does it have to be me?"

"Oh, go on," Kat said sweetly, "You're small, and you're the fastest.
You can do it!" she purred, as she batted her eyelashes.

Melrose suddenly grew bold; he pumped his little chest.
And off he ran to bravely try to do his best.
While they sat there for a rest, up against a rock,
Melrose ran ahead to do his mission for the flock.

Before he got too far, he thought he smelled a fire.
No sooner did he blink before he sensed something dire.
He heard a sound and froze, danger tickling his nose,
His ears perked up as tiny cries of capture rose.

Silently, he scanned the dark dirt path up ahead.
What emerged before his eyes filled him full of dread!
Front and center was a bobcat, crouched sleek and low.
His eyes were scary fierce with a dangerous yellow.

By his paw, a mouse screeched; a look of horror on his face.
The bobcat had its tail firmly locked in place.
But Melrose caught his eye, and then, in a flash,
The bobcat turned around, about to make a dash.

The mouse ran away; the bobcat showed no care.
For now it seemed the squirrel made for meatier fare.
Melrose feared for his life, and took off in flight,
Back toward the group, huddled closely in the night.
The bobcat gave swift chase, closing in on his prey,
Until he reached the clearing, where the other's lay.

They collided forcefully. The bobcat let out a wail.
Kat shrieked angrily, "HEY! You made me break a nail!
You big OAF!" she snapped his way, "Are you BLIND? Can't you SEE?"
The bobcat cowered meekly, "I, um, well, uh, please forgive me . . ."
Melrose sat there stunned, stuck between these two.
"Well, we'll see," Kat shot back, "What sort of cat ARE you?"
"Name's Beardsley, Miss, a bobcat. The only one here."
He shook the stars from his eyes until his vision was clear.

"You have WHITE in your eyes!" Kat cried with surprise.
"All the others have these mean and buggy, WEIRD, yellow eyes!"
"Yes, that's true," Beardsley sighed, "Part of the Tribal Ring;
All the yellow that you saw, they're all the Eyes of The King."

"The Eyes of The King?" they all asked at once.
"That's right," Beardsley answered, "That's how the King hunts.
They all work together, as part of his tribe;
When they see something strange, they send each other a vibe."

They looked at him, skeptically; then Wiggleworm laughed,
"So the worm that yelled at me, you mean, is on the King's staff?"
Sammy chimed in, "Well, he WAS Royal Blue!"
Watching them all giggling made Beardsley laugh too.

"I know it must sound silly, but you need to beware.
Stick with me; I'll make sure to keep you out of their stare.
Come with me to where I camp; it's not that far from here."
So off they went with their new friend, and without fear.

"Okay, here we are! This is home, sweet home!
It's not much, I'm afraid, but then I've always been alone . . ."

"Is that a cave I see?" Wiggleworm asked nervously.
Sammy backed away from its mouth, carefully.

"Yes, would you like to see?" Beardsley asked cheerfully.
"Um, no that's okay," Sammy muttered quietly.

Kat began to chuckle, "Does it have any bats?
'Cause that's what Sammy's used to; maybe even some rats?"

Melrose chimed in, "You should have seen your face!
You were running so fast, you could have won a race!"

"So you found the bat cave," Beardsley winked with a smile.
"Been there, done that! I think they chased me for a MILE!"
This made Sammy smile, "You mean YOU were SCARED?"
Beardsley said, "No . . . I was 'SCAREDER' than scared!"

Their laughter seemed as bright as the stars above.
The night sounds were softened by the cooing of a dove.
Beardsley made a fire from a stick and a stone,
"I don't remember laughing all these years I've been alone."

So now they had their camp, and all the warmth it would bring.
They soon forgot about the eerie Eyes of The King.
As the five sat quietly, the fire grew warm and bright.
Together they were safe; it would be a good night.

Salty Splashes

C O L L E C T I O N™

Salty Splashes

COLLECTION™